Usborne

a·b·c

Sticker & Colouring Book

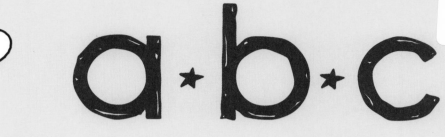

Illustrated by Stacey Lamb
Designed by Claire Ever

You'll find all the stickers in
the middle of the book.

a

b

astronaut

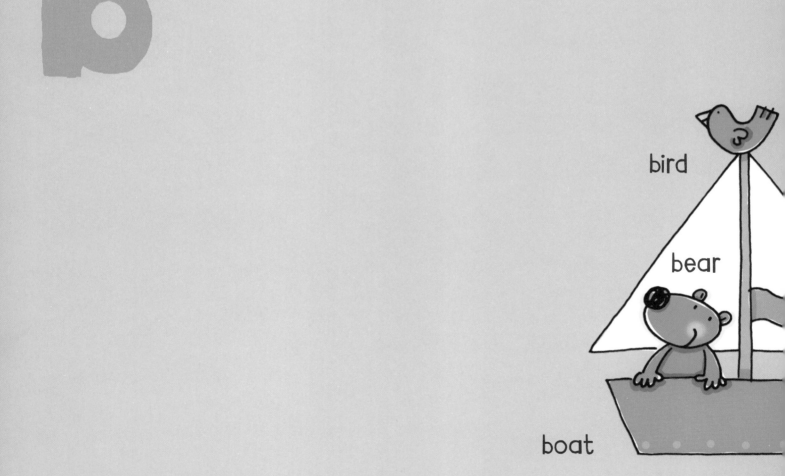

bird

bear

boat

a b c d e f g h i j k l r

C

cat

car

cow

n o p q r s t u v w x y z

d

dog

digger

e

elephant

f

flower

o p q r s t u v w x y z

g

giraffe

h

house

a b c d e f **g** **h** **i** **j** k l r

i

island

j

jigsaw puzzle

n o p q r s t u v w x y z

k

kite

l

lion

m

moon

n

nest

n o p q r s t u v w x y z

o

octopus

p

present

q

queen

r

rabbit

rocket

o p q r s t u v w x y z

star

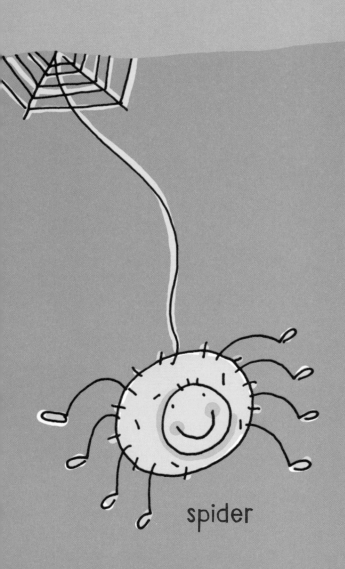

spider

a b c d e f g h i j k l n

t

tree

train

tiger

n o p q r s **s** **t** u v w x y z

U

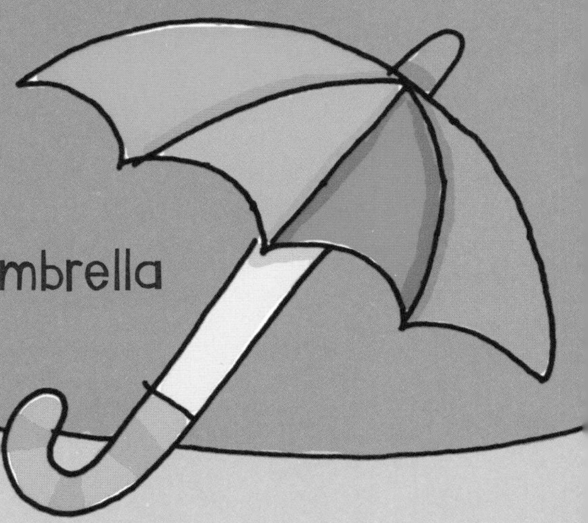

V

W

umbrella

water

a b c d e f g h i j k l r

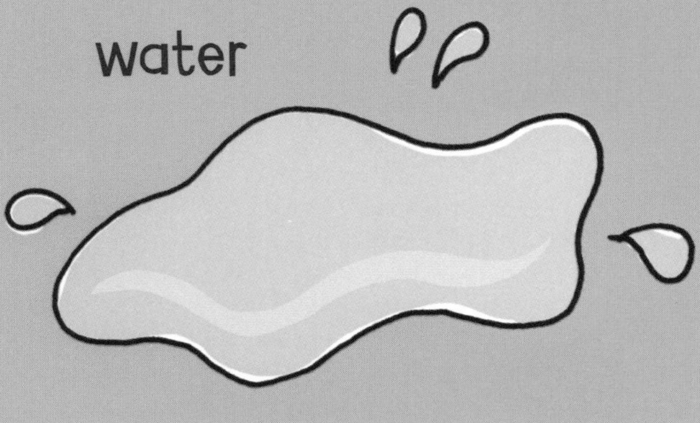

a b c

asleep

bicycle

caterpillar

butterfly

carrot

apron

boy

ball

bucket

bee

ant

cloud

clock

balloon

castle

x

y

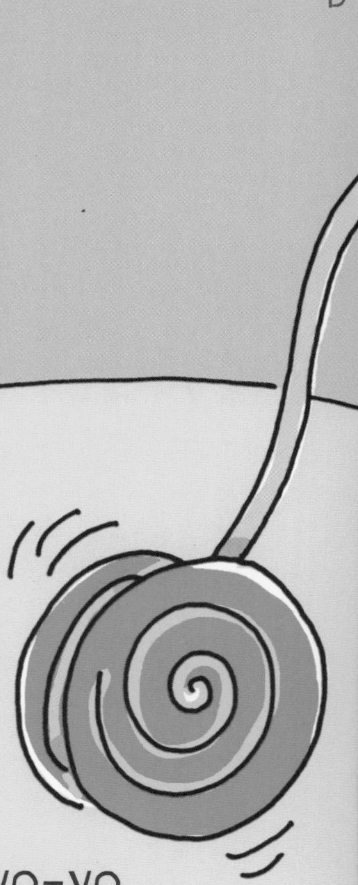

yo-yo

z

zebra

n o p q r s t u v w x y z

Find the picture stickers to match the letters.

apple

Bb

Cc

dinosaur

Ee

Ff

Gg

hat

Hh

Ii

jacket

Kk

Ll

mouse

Mm

Nn

Oo

Pp

Qq

Rr

Ss

Tt

Uu

Vv

Ww

Xx

Yy

Zz

d e f

fairy

eat

farmer

doll

donkey

door

fire engine

egg

frog

earth

duck

dress

dolphin

fish

g h i j

helicopter

juice

gloves

insect

girl

hen

jam

gate

ice cream

grapes

ink

horse

k l m n o

leaf

net

monkey

lamb

mirror

lemon

lamp

nurse

kitten

keys

king

kick

necklace

o p q r

penguin

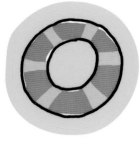
painting

radio

owl

onion

quack!

ring

robot

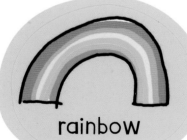
rainbow

rose

quarter

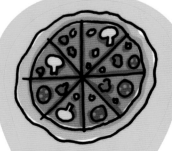
orange

pizza

parrot

s t

ship

table

tortoise

sandwich

teddy bear

sun

tractor

sock

toothbrush

skirt

snail

tomato

strawberry

snake

tent

truck

Stickers for pages 14–15

upside down

vegetables

x-ray

yogurt

whistle

wheelbarrow

yellow

undress

vet

xylophone

zigzag

watch

vase

window

zoo

yawn

apple

butterfly

castle

dinosaur

elephant

frog

grapes

helicopter

ink

juice

kite

leaf

mouse

net

octopus

parrot

queen

robot

snake

tree

umbrella

vegetables

watch

xylophone

yo-yo

zebra

Colouring

In this part of the book, there are lots of pictures to colour.

a

ant

apple

b

butterfly

ball

boat

c

cat

car

castle

d

dog

digger

e

elephant

f

fish

flower

g

girl

gate

house

h

hat

i

insects

ink

j

jeans

jacket

k

kite

kick

l

lion

leaf

m

mouse

moon

n

nest

octopus

o

p

penguins

s

sun

sandcastle

t

tent

tiger

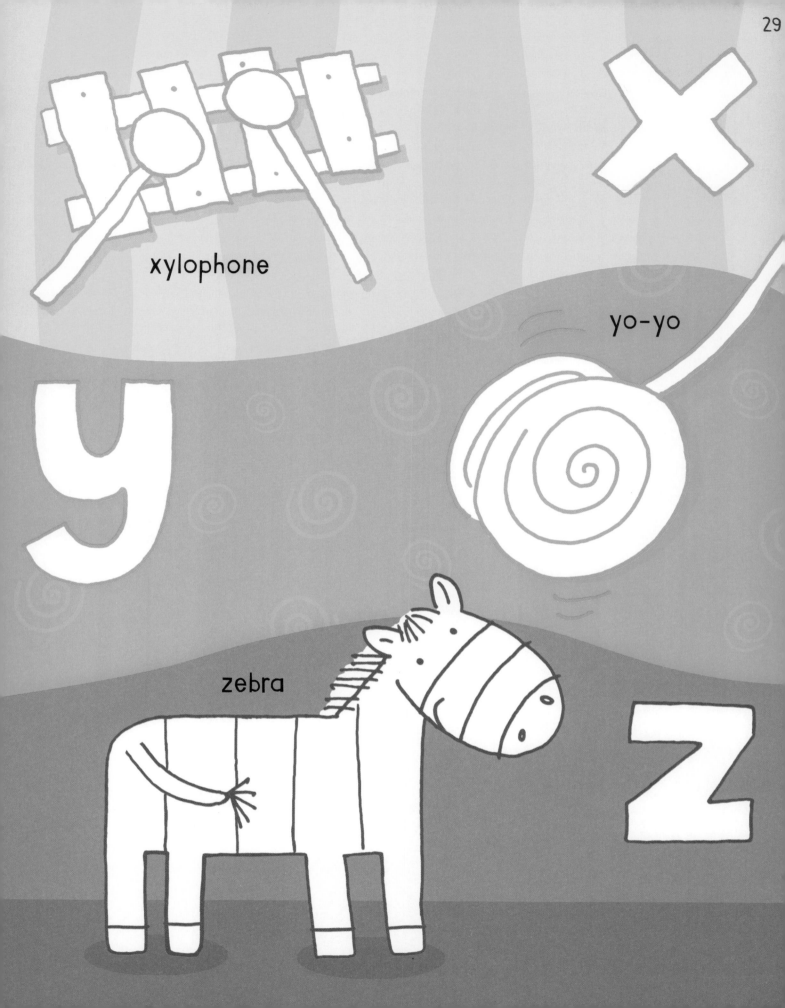

xylophone

x

yo-yo

y

zebra

z

30 Colour the pictures.

apple

boat

cat

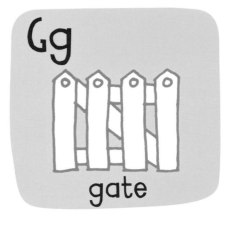
gate

house

insect

moon

nest

octopus

sun

tiger

umbrella

Dd

digger

Ee

elephant

Ff

fish

Jj

jacket

Kk

kite

Ll

leaf

Pp

penguin

Qq

quack!

Rr

rocket

Vv

vegetables

Ww

woof!

Xx
xylophone

Yy

yo-yo

Zz
zebra

Colour the letters.